LITTLE MISS MUFFET

Little Miss Muffet
Sat on a tuffet,
Eating her curds and whey;
There came a big spider,
Who sat down beside her
And frightened Miss Muffet away.

MARY HAD A LITTLE LAMB

Mary had a little lamb,
Its fleece was white as snow;
And everywhere that Mary went,
The lamb was sure to go.

BAA, BAA, BLACK SHEEP

Baa, baa, black sheep,
Have you any wool?
Yes, sir, yes,
Three bags

LITTLE BOY BLUE

Little Boy Blue, come blow your horn!
The sheep's in the meadow, the cow's in the corn.
Where's the little boy that looks after the sheep?
Under the haystack, fast asleep!

THE HOUSE THAT JACK BUILT

This is the house that Jack built.
This is the malt
That lay in the house that Jack built.
This is the rat,
That ate the malt
That lay in the house that Jack built.

THE LION AND THE UNICORN

The lion and the unicorn
Were fighting for the crown;
The lion beat the unicorn
All around the town.

THERE WAS A CROOKED MAN

There was a crooked man
And he went a crooked mile,
He found a crooked sixpence
Beside a crooked stile.

THERE WAS AN OLD WOMAN WHO LIVED IN A SHOE

There was an old woman who lived in a shoe,
She had so many children she didn't know what to do.
She gave them some broth without any bread:
She whipped them all soundly and put them to bed.

THE CAT AND THE FIDDLE

Hey diddle, diddle!
The cat and the fiddle,
The cow jumped over the moon;
The little dog laughed
To see such sport,
And the dish ran away with the spoon.

BANBURY CROSS

Ride a cock-horse to Banbury Cross,
To see an old lady upon a white horse.
Rings on her fingers, and bells on her toes,
She shall have music wherever she goes.

WEE WILLIE WINKIE

Wee Willie Winkie runs through the town,
Upstairs and downstairs, in his nightgown;
Rapping at the window, crying through the lock,
'Are the children in their beds? Now it's eight o'clock!'

THE THREE LITTLE KITTENS

Three little kittens
They lost their mittens,
And they began to cry,
'Oh, mother dear,
We sadly fear
Our mittens we have lost.'

HUSH-A-BYE

Hush-a-bye, baby on the tree top!
When the wind blows the cradle will rock;
When the bough breaks the cradle will fall,
Down will come baby, cradle, and all.

This book was given to

. . . .

with love from

. . . .

For the wonderful Mrs Wilton – MS
For Sean, Morgan and Oliver – JL

©2005 The Chicken House

This edition first published in the United Kingdom in 2005 by
The Chicken House, 2 Palmer Street, Frome, Somerset, BA11 1DS
www.doublecluck.com

Text © 2005 Mark Sperring
Illustrations © 2005 Jonathan Langley

Designed by Ian Butterworth

Printed and bound in Singapore

British Library Cataloguing in Publication Data available
Library of Congress Cataloguing in Publication Data available

Hardback ISBN 1 904442 45 5
Paperback ISBN 1 904442 69 2

The Fairytale Cake

Made by Jonathan Langley

from a Recipe by Mark Sperring

The Chicken HOUSE

We make a cake,

we bake a cake,

a very, very special cake,

and send it on its way.

Up the hill

and down the hill,

across the bridge,

and through the fields,

rolling, rolling, rolling,

rolling on its way.

Here it comes, that special cake.

That very, very special cake.

So close your eyes,

and make a wish!

Happy, Happy Birthday!

THE QUEEN OF HEARTS

The Queen of Hearts,
She made some tarts,
All on a summer's day;
The Knave of Hearts,
He stole the tarts,
And took them clean away.

PAT-A-CAKE

Pat-a-cake, pat-a-cake,
Bake me a cake as fast as you can!
Pat it and prick it, and mark it with B
Put it in the oven for Baby and me!

SING A SONG OF SIXPENCE

Sing a song of sixpence,
A pocket full of rye;
Four-and-twenty blackbirds
Baked in a pie!

LITTLE JACK HORNER

Little Jack Horner
Sat in the corner,
Eating of Christmas pie:
He put in his thumb,
And pulled out a plum,
And said, 'What a good boy am I!'

LITTLE TOMMY TUCKER

Little Tommy Tucker,
Sings for his supper.
What shall we give him?
White bread and butter.

POLLY, PUT THE KETTLE ON

Polly, put the kettle on,
Polly, put the kettle on,
Polly, put the kettle on,
And let's drink tea.

OLD MOTHER HUBBARD

Old Mother Hubbard,
Went to the cupboard,
To give her poor dog a bone;
But when she got there,
The cupboard was bare,
And so the poor dog had none.

OLD KING COLE

Old King Cole
Was a merry old soul,
And a merry old soul was he;
He called for his pipe,
And he called for his bowl,
And he called for his fiddlers three!

LITTLE BO-PEEP

Little Bo-Peep has lost her sheep,
And can't tell where to find them;
Leave them alone, and they'll come home,
And bring their tails behind them.

OH, THE GRAND OLD DUKE OF YORK

Oh, the grand old Duke of York,
He had ten thousand men;
He marched them up to the top of the hill,
And he marched them down again.

JACK AND JILL

Jack and Jill went up the hill,
To fetch a pail of water;
Jack fell down and broke his crown,
And Jill came tumbling after.

DING, DONG, BELL

Ding, dong, bell,
Pussy's in the well!
Who put her in?
Little Tommy Lin.

RUB-A-DUB-DUB

Rub-a-dub-dub,
Three men in a tub,
And how do you think they got there?
The butcher, the baker,
The candlestick-maker,
They all jumped out of a rotten potato!

HUMPTY DUMPTY

Humpty Dumpty sat on a wall,
Humpty Dumpty had a great fall;
All the King's horses, and all the King's men
Couldn't put Humpty together again.

I SAW THREE SHIPS

I saw three ships come sailing by,
I saw three ships come sailing by,
Come sailing by, come sailing by,
I saw three ships come sailing by,
On New-Year's day in the morning.